Summer With A Ranger

A Texan Devils undercover summer fling

Sofia Aves

EBOOK ISBN 978-1-922448-72-9

PRINT ISBN 978-1-923471-06-1

Hudson Wittington never thought he'd leave the LA Fire Dept. to cross the country and accept a trial position in an elite Texas Ranger's unit that includes undercover work in Tijuana. But that's where he finds himself when a beach babe decides to use him as her personal bodyguard to ward off undesirables for the remainder of his trip.

It should be an easy job—both of them. But before he heads back to Texas, Hudson learns a few home truths about himself, and he might have given away his heart to a woman he isn't sure wants to risk hers on him in the process.

Because sex on the beach isn't just a drink

CHAPTER ONE

HUSDON

One week into my job as the newest recruit in Rhys Archer's elite Texas Ranger Unit out of Austin and I was sitting on a beach in Tijuana, sipping cocktails decorated with pretty umbrellas and plastic red cherries.

Hudson Whittington, Texas Ranger.

Who would have thought it?

It wasn't a bad way to start a new job, if I didn't say so myself. Not only did I pull undercover work as my first assignment, but I also got to wrangle the floating eye candy tourist population for a solid seven days.

My first wasn't a long assignment, but I knew the gig for what it was: a test.

Make contact, get the product, and swan around for a full week. Don't trip yourself up, and don't break your cover. Come back home when you're done.

Those were the rules I was given to earn a shiny brass star and a white hat. My sandbox to play in. Do the job, and do it well, or haul my ass back to California where I spent the last nine years as a fixture in the LA Fire Department.

I'd never had a problem with my career choices and I loved my job, but now that Archer had given me a taste of what I could do on this side of the border, I wasn't sure I could go back.

Which made this a pass/fail task with an ultimatum at the other end. It was kind of easier, to be fair.

And three days into my allocated time on the beach, I was halfway there. I made the contact, tasted drugs for the second time in my life—the first time during college and I fucking hated the lack of control over my body and thoughts—and made a faux friend for life in my Tijuana dealer, Tag. The name had a ... nice ring to it. I was scheduled to pick up the product I was supposed to pretend to distribute back home in Cali in a few days, then head home.

Only if I had my way, I wasn't going back to

Cali. Austin, Texas, would be my new/old-to-me baseline. The dirt I grew up tasting.

Memories of my childhood attempted to flood back: the house I used to live in, the family that fell apart. That was how I ended up on a different side of the country. My chest closed at the emotional deluge I rejected on sight, and I sucked in a long, slow breath.

Not the time. Or the place.

Because right now I had a date with a beach.

I sank into the divot my body made in my borrowed beach towel, the sand accommodating my mass gracefully, heating my back in the sun-warmed sand. It wasn't midday yet, and the extra endorphins already flooded my body. Being a Texas Ranger might not be like this every day, but right now, I'd take it.

Of course, the singular doubt in my gut remained that maybe I wasn't as worthy as Archer thought.

Walking into his office was the singularly most nerve wracking thing I'd ever done. The quiet man with rust coloured hair and a scarred face stared across the desk at me while I tried not to fidget like a teenage kid called in to see the principal.

I'd always been proud of being a firefighter, but that career choice seemed flimsy the moment I walked into the Austin unit's office. The space was filled with men in pressed shirts and white hats, that little star badge displayed somewhere on their person.

Dressed in faded jeans, boots I did up at the entrance foyer, and an old gray LA Fire Dept. tee, I stood out in the worst of ways.

Not that I felt lesser in any physical sense; I was more than a match for the team in terms of muscle and height, but ego wise... I was born and bred in Texas and made the move to LA chasing sun and surf.

And a little excitement.

Those career choices got me laid, paid and in front of Archer, or at least that was what he told me. How he picked me out of the population of previous and current Texan residents I couldn't say, only that I was grateful for the chance.

That, and my intention not to fuck up.

That seed of doubt dissipated with a fine spray of sand and salt water dripping on me. I cracked one eye open to find a visage of tanned and toned skin in a sapphire blue bikini standing before me in a sarong. One muscular thigh slipped out from beneath the gold and blue filmy material.

The girl perched on her towel she placed right

beside me, closer than any stranger should be, drop dead stunning or not. My stomach tensed, and not by design, just from her proximity. One slim arm reached out behind her. She arched her back slightly with one leg bent, and the other straight out as she looked down at the imperiously.

"You're my bodyguard for the next four days."

"I'm your what?" I raised both eyebrows and tried not to waggle them, but holy *shit* on a beach ball was she gorgeous. "I didn't know they made them like you in Tijuana."

She smirked, nary a giggle in sight, flicking beachy blonde waves over her shoulder. Everything about this woman was hard, in a goddess sort of way. From the set of her mouth to the fiery blaze behind deep blue eyes, her straight spine, the way she sat... everything was utter perfection to my eyes.

Except maybe that golden hair that reminded me of California.

In one fell swoop I was home sick.

Setting my teeth, I flexed both arms, tucking them behind my head and closed my eyes. I couldn't work out what was hotter: her gaze, or the sun.

"I've got a deadline, and I need protection from this." Her tone bordered on derisive. I kept my eyes closed but imagined her waving a hand at the remainder of the population on the beach. "You'll stop them from hitting on me."

"What makes you think anyone wants to hit on you?" I was glad my eyes stayed shut. After that snappy little repartee, I fully expected a slap in the face.

Sand flicked on my stomach, and I managed not to flinch. *Just.*

"Asshole," she said idly. "What's your name?"

"Hudson. Whittington." I managed around a thick tongue that didn't' feel like it belonged in my mouth, and cracked an eye open.

"Skye Gallagher." She held out a hand, complete with callouses, and short, French polished tips.

The best of both worlds. A Queen, if rough at a few hidden edges. I liked what I saw already, though I knew she'd be a ballbuster. Knowing she worked with her hands sometimes, even if it was sport or around the yard, lit something inside me. I wanted to see her sweat. I wanted to see her get filthy and lick her clean.

Where they fuck did that come from?

I had a job to do, for fuck's sake. But still, a little eye candy and a summer fantasy could be fun to indulge in. Plus, her proposition fit my cover. *Yeah. That works.*

I pulled my head out of my cock and bullshit long enough to respond to her.

"That's apt."

"How's that?" She stared at me imperiously through narrowed, slitted eyes.

"Gallagher. It means *stranger*. Or warrior. Depends which side of the internet you believe."

"How do you know that?"

"I grew up living next door to some Gallaghers. Good neighbors."

"Funny, that." Her eyes softened, the tiniest bit, or maybe I imagined it. "Now stay, Huddy boy, and look pretty."

Who said I was staying?

But we both knew I would. I kept the wince off my face at the shitty nickname all the same.

"Yes, ma'am."

After that she stayed silent while my mind wandered. I was halfway through a damn fine daydream about toned thighs and a blue bikini that matched her blue eyes when a finger poked me in the ribs.

"Wake up, baby oil boy. You're turning lobster red."

"I am?" I cracked open an eye and looked down at my chest, spotting nothing but a bronzed plateau that matched hers, albeit with less curves. "I don't see what you're seeing."

"Clearly not." That smirk was back in her voice.

"So, I'm your bodyguard." I mean, who was I to say no to a pretty woman? Besides, my job was to stay low. Look like an overgrown kid out for fun and sun and maybe a few drugs. The thought of her believing that story hit me square in the guts, and I pushed it aside. "Who says we're staying the same length of time?"

"I'm here for a few days. Not sure." Skye shifted beside me as I raised up onto my elbows, cracking my neck. She winced. "Ouch."

"Yeah, that wasn't the best." I rubbed the back of my neck. "Where are you staying?" She rattled off the name of the quaint little beach cottage Archer booked for me, a word I hadn't been able to pronounce since I arrived. "Oh, good. We're staying in the same place," I said dryly.

The tiny little cottage had eight rooms, each seemingly smaller than the last, but it was cute, across the road from the beach, and it was two doors up from my new bestie, Tag the mini drug lord.

"Perfect." She smiled, and her face lit up in a whole new way. "Staying till Sunday?"

"Yeah." I pretended not to be floored but might have drooled on her a little.

Damn, a girl with her own mind, knowing what she wanted and who looked like that? Ticked all my boxes, straight up.

Still, I was supposed to be working. Four days I was going to be paired with this girl? I mean, I could haul my ass off the beach and leave her to it any time. She wasn't quite the type of damsel in distress I was used to rescuing. But seeing as I had some spare time...

"I do have shit to do here, you know."

"I'll be fine while you do your manly stuff. Anyway, baby oil boy, or whatever you use. You're gonna look like a lobster by dinner."

"Yes, ma'am," I said resignedly, hiding my own smirk, thinking back on her introduction. "What's your deadline for?"

"Creative nonfiction."

What the fuck is that?

She raised an eyebrow. "Eloquent. Maybe you can be my test subject."

"I– what?" I shook my head, rubbing sunscreen on my face and the rest of me.

Her azure gaze tracked an appreciative line down my body that stirred my blood. I returned the favor, leaving my attention to wander over her toned calves and stomach with that sexy goddamn line down the middle. The girl put some serious hours into working her body beautifully for her to look like that. I was just there to appreciate it.

"You really don't have a filter, do you?" She laughed at me, bringing me back.

Golden waves settled almost to her waist in long, oversized curls, looking natural as hell. Actually, everything about her looked natural, which was a bit of a relief. Living in LA meant there was a whole lot of fake going on, and I'd never been able to stomach it. Tits with implants just didn't feel right in my hands.

She laughed outright, and my mouth snapped shut.

I gave her a crooked smile. "Nope. No filtered fucks served here."

"Good. Maybe you can call me out with my bull-shit if it gets too much."

I raised both eyebrows. She seemed real about it, but who knew. Maybe I'd get to test that out some time. Four days with this girl and we'd be driving each other fucking nuts. She was clearly a profes-sional of whatever creativeness she delved into. I was more the laid back sort, happy with my ass in the sand and making sure everyone around me was safe.

Still, she was sexy as hell, and I did have time on my hands.

"I can do that," I hedged, wondering what the hell I just signed up for.

I straightened, wrapping my arms around my knees and looked out over the water. The glorious morning merged into an afternoon filled with dark clouds across the horizon. Tendrils of out of season fog preceding the oncoming storm crept across the water.

"Looks like you want to pack that up, princess." The last rays of sun soaked my back with glorious heat. *Here's hoping for more assignments over the border.* "So, what's this creative thing?" I scratched my brow, trying to remember what she said.

Skye jerked, staring at the encroaching wall of water, and I didn't mean the surf sort. "Shit." The girl swore liberally as she packed her things, earning a few glances from other beachgoers as they collected their belongings, trudging back up the still-warm sand.

"Walk you back to the cottage? I think we're staying at the same place." I repeated myself as I folded my towel and stuffed one hand into my pocket.

"Thanks." Not beating around the bush, she swung an oversized beach tote onto her shoulder with everything stuffed inside, including a pale pink laptop case decorated with gold swirls all over it.

"Cute." I offered her an easy smile. I hoped. When she shot me a raised eyebrow and a disapproving look, I waved a hand feebly at her bag. "Laptop case. It's pretty."

Great grasp on the English language right there.

"No filter, and not smooth. Glad you've got muscles going for you, big boy." She tapped my shoulder and strode ahead of me. Each step was sure in the sand, her toned calf muscles tensing with each step as she plowed her way toward the street.

"Maybe a heart to match," I murmured to her back.

I kept my eyes fixed straight ahead and rolled my shoulders. Welp. At least the last few days of my trip wouldn't be wasted. I could perfect some of that lacking charm that the rest of the unit had going on before I walked back in the door and claimed my badge on Monday.

Keeping my eyes fixed firmly ahead I couldn't

help my gaze wandering towards the perfect pair of hips that swayed gently as she walked.

Okay, so I lied to myself earlier. Not everything was hard about her.

CHAPTER TWO

HUDSON

"You'll get your product." Tag, the Mexican dealer contact Archer sent me to find nodded, his arms folded over his chest. "When I can confirm who you are from California. Got a few connections there I might check in with, seeing as you're new blood to the area and all." Sweat glistened on his pock-marked face as he leered at me.

I tried not to look at the sores decorating his skin, or the decay in his mouth when he offered me a too-wide smile and an expulsion of tepid air.

My stomach turned as I eyed the plethora of designer drugs laid out on the folding table in several assorted baggies, trying not to belay my disquiet. *Here's hoping Archer's got someone good on the other side of the country.* Because if the dude looked me up, he'd find a fairly clean man with no criminal history and no trust factor, leaving me a buck shy of the drugs I was meant to take back to Texas.

"Take your time." I leaned against the doorway, scratching my shoulders on the hard ridge, and tried not to panic.

Breathe. Archer wouldn't have sent you in if he didn't have faith in you.

Or backed me up. Unless there was an initiation ceremony I missed.

A slightly smaller man with dark hair perched at the other end of the short table counting money and drinking straight from the tequila bottle at his side. The man had a barrel chest that looked like he could cripple a bear with a one-armed stranglehold.

"Got some friends in SoCal, we do." Tag turned to the man counting his money. "Don't we, Angel?"

Angel nodded, not raising his head from his counting and scribbling something on a pad beside him. I took in as much detail about the room as I possibly could. What sort of weapons they both carried, the size of the stacks of bills on the table, and the number of drugs in their possession.

I knew narcotics tracking was a huge part of Archer's unit and prevented them from entering the

US. That and human trafficking seemed to be his main focus from the short rundown I got in his office.

That was five days ago, and it suddenly seemed like months.

Angel offered me the tequila. I took the bottle with some small reservations, wiping the lip with my shirt and slugged two solid mouthfuls before handing it back. The Patrón burned its way down my throat and numbed my lips.

Angel didn't so much as look up as I handed the bottle back, but I could swear the man smiled.

"So, who you gonna call?" I lifted my lips at my own joke, though Tag looked at me curiously. I shook my head. "It doesn't matter. I'm heading back in a few days. Had a long damn night." I tacked on the information that wasn't entirely false.

I spent the night watching the storm roll through and a pair of long legs that appeared over my veranda at the back of the cottage, the sounds of the beach filtering through the still night. Turned out my beach babe took the room next to mine. She had perfect toes and perfect feet too, setting off a fetish I didn't know I had until then.

Skye. I discovered her name on my second day on bodyguard duty at the beach. Not that she said much to me since then. My time in this shithole of a building was almost up, and I was determined to at least get myself a decent kiss from the girl, refusing to leave Tijuana without one.

I inclined my head, trying to focus back on my job and not perky tits and pink painted toenails that matched her laptop case.

Fuck me. Or her. Either way, I was good with it.

I shifted discreetly to adjust my reaction to the thought. "Anyway. Let me know if you want me to take anything back, or when I head back next time I'm down."

Tag looked at me sharply. "You said take your time."

I shrugged again. "You can take all the time you want. This trip, next trip, whatever. I ain't going anywhere."

"Except back to SoCal," Angel broke his silence.

I nodded. "Except for that."

Tag folded his arms, his fingers jittering against his ribs. A side effect of using his own drugs? "Come back tomorrow," he said finally.

"Yes, ma'am." I ducked out the door before he realized what I said.

As I whipped out of the building, I could've sworn Angel smiled again.

I shouldn't have asked to read what she wrote.

That was all that crossed my mind as I stared down at the sexist gibberish that covered the digital page. Mind, seeing as she used a stranger to keep her single status card intact, I shouldn't have been surprised. Still, those words actually did reduce her sex appeal.

Minutely, maybe.

Fuck it. I still wanted that kiss.

Girls, if you're going to free air the kitty to encourage your man into action, he might need a little help. Flick the skirt, grind, let his hand wander. Sometimes men can be so ingrained in their habits they usually can't see what's right in front of them. But keep it discreet. Subtle is sexy.

I blinked at the screen. What were we, men from the stone ages? Miss Skye Hamilton–I stalked her name and maybe her number in the cottage guest book–needed a little nudge in the right direction. Setting my jaw, I handed her laptop back, ready to rain hell on her thoughts about my sex.

"You might wanna go easy on the, uh, aggressive

tone," I murmured, trying to work out how not to offend her while still getting my point across.

"You don't like men being objectified the way you have with women for centuries?" She tossed her glorious mane over her shoulder, a defiant glint in her eye that may or may not have bordered on maniacal.

"Damn, that's pretty. Huh?" I half reached out to touch her, though my hand suddenly stung like hell. "I didn't deserve that." I looked at her after studying the pink finger marks on the back of my hand. *Really* looked at her, and reassessed my original vision of the girl who wouldn't leave me alone.

Strong, but fragile underneath. She's covering cracks in her self-belief with muscle so she can fight what—who—ever comes at her.

Nothing about my epiphany made her less sexy in my eyes. Maybe more so, because now I knew she wasn't just driven, she was also a fighter.

"You did."

"Nope. Just stating what I see, princess."

"See." She flicked sand at me. The golden grains bounced off her laptop case. "Objectifying me."

"Yeah, just like you did the first day you planted your tush beside me—unobjectified tush—" I held up a finger when her pretty mouth opened—the objectified, pretty mouth I wanted to do bad, bad things to–and kept talking. "–and called me baby oil boy, and big boy, saying I had nothing going for me but muscles." Okay, so I paraphrased, but that was the gist of it.

Her mouth opened, and closed, then opened again. "That's not–"

"What you meant to say, but it is what happened," I reminded her gently. "Maybe you should look inside with this one, Skye, before you send that off to wherever it's going."

Personal blog, her friends group, a magazine, what the fuck ever. But she'd get blasted for it, or I had no faith in the female population standing up for their favorite boy toys, and not the battery operated sort.

"How dare you." She crossed her arms over her chest. "Do you understand why I word things the way I do?"

"Enlighten me."

"You're ridiculously white," she seethed. I raised an eyebrow and gestured at her Aryan look. She ignored me. "*Privileged* may as well be stamped across your forehead. Or maybe it's on the back of your designer polo."

"You're wearing the same label as me." I pointed

out, unwilling to back down just because her bikini bottoms got in a sexy, damp little twist.

"Hudson, let me mansplain this one for you." She ran her fingers through her hair. "I reach women in all corners of the US, and some farther afield. Some are very quiet, conservative areas. Some aren't white areas." The obsessive—excuse me, *passionate*—gleam replaced a flicker of exhaustion in her gaze, lifting the color in her face. "Let's say we went out on a date. We got along well, shared a hot kiss, and decided to take it further. Both of us being professional city dwellers, or wherever you come from. Would you think less of me in the morning for it?"

How long were you up writing for last night, Skye? Because she sure as hell outlasted me when I dozed in my chair for half the night, creating new fantasies about my beach towel buddy.

Her gaze fixed on me, and a flush travelled up my cheeks. I resisted the urge to curve my hand around her nape, pull her into me, and find out just what that scenario she outlined felt like first hand.

"Of course not."

The image of kissing her hard enough to push her against a wall in my room and run my hands up those toned thighs and beneath her sarong ripped through my mind on a swift current of searing arousal.

My cheeks weren't the only things overheating.

"Good." She smiled, and there was heat in her gaze, too. "Let's go back to those country areas. If those women suddenly did a lap dance for their very conservative partner, they could be labelled as sluts, abused, or thrown out. Certainly some would become homeless or humiliated. Maybe..." Her smile faded but her gaze remained intense. She didn't finish her sentence, and she didn't need to.

Point made.

I clenched my teeth. "I get that. But it's–"

"You do. Really?"

"Really, Skye. I do. It's making a man feel so objectified reading those words. The language. Where's the love and attraction between your couple in that scenario?" I searched her face this time, my palms pressed to my board shorts. Designer, sure. But only because they came from the closest shop in Texas when I was offered the job on a time trial basis.

"Oh. My. You are, aren't you?" She shot me a false eye roll and a snarky little smirk I wanted to kiss right off her face. "You're a romantic. For fuck's sake, Hudson. Grow up. The world is here for what we take, to make us feel better for our shortcomings. Let me assure you no woman will be happy with everything you do. Love doesn't work that way." Her short speech ended on a decisively bitter tang.

I pushed her laptop aside on her tote, leaned forward, and braced an arm over her head on her towel, forcing her to lean back or end up pressed chest to chest with me. Close enough to breathe in her lilies and dewdrops scent. Romantic? Hell, yes. I was a tragic, and I'd cling to that and my man card on my way to hell or my grave one day, whichever came first. No way was I stopping just because...

Skye stared at me through hooded eyes half-covered by thick lashes I wanted to brush my mouth over, and breathe her in. The need in me was reflected in her mirrored gaze. In her dilated pupils. But there was something more there...deeper than desire, something a little darker...

I swore inside my head, and touched her lips tenderly with aching fingers, wishing I'd figured her out that much sooner. Taken a risk that much sooner. "Who hurt you so bad you can't wear rose tinted glasses for a single moment, Skye?" I brushed my fingers over her cheek, guiding a stray golden strand behind her ear.

She squeaked, and pressed her hands to my

chest, though she didn't push me away. At all. "Don't touch me. Those things aren't real, Hudson." She slipped out from under me, already packing her things into her beach tote, her hands busy as she talked.

Hiding.

She shot me a fragile look, both filled with anger that I'd uncovered her secret and something...more, right before she took off across the beach, her sandals dangling from her fingers and spraying sand everywhere.

My chest closed again. *I shouldn't have said anything.* Should I? Fuck, I had no idea. But I couldn't leave her hurting like that, not when I was the one responsible for upsetting her.

Yeah, that sounded as good a reason as any.

I grabbed my towel, and something hit my foot. Something sharp with metal edges. I collected her purse, tucking the overfilled thing with cards and change and a star necklace poking out at all angles from it, and chased her across the road, darting between pedestrians and finally catching her in the hallway of the cottage.

"Damn, you move fast," I huffed, not really out of breath but startled she nearly out ran me. I got no answer as she shoved her door–*her unlocked door, what the actual fuck?*–open with trembling hands.

Taking the risk I probably shouldn't, I followed her in, closing and locking her door behind me. "Skye, I'm–"

"You shouldn't be in here." She stared at me with a blank face, all the roiling emotion of a moment before completely gone.

I blinked at her. Angry Skye, I could manage, even if she irritated the shit out of me. Derisive, snobby Skye, even fragile Skye. But blank Skye? Nope. Seeing her close off like that broke something inside me.

Swallowing hard, I held out her purse. "You left this."

She stared at me for a second, then caught the pink thing that matched her laptop case. Cursing myself internally as an utter asshole I let her take it, using the movement to circle her wrist in my hand loosely, stopping her retreat.

"Wait."

"No."

My eyes shut and I let her go.

Silence fell in the room.

"Just like that?" Her voice trembled a little.

I opened my eyes. "Just like that."

"You won't fight for what you want?" Blue eyes bored into mine like she could pierce my fucking soul.

"I'll never force a woman," I corrected her, my voice straining. My hands fisted at my sides, and I turned away from her. "Be safe, Skye."

"You're all the things I didn't write about." Surprise filled her voice.

Rolling my lips together, I squeezed them hard, and turned back. *Keep on walking, Hudson. Right out her door.* Naturally, I ignored that wise little voice. Why break a lifetime habit?

"Yeah, you're not writing about men like me. The ones with hearts, whether they wear them on their sleeves, or hide them away for that special life partner who respects them." I took a step closer, and she didn't move. "The men who revere their woman, who don't want anything more than to come home, spend time with her, and make sure her day wasn't a shit fight, even if his was. To give her everything." My voice cracked and I gave a hollow laugh, still closing the distance between us step by step. "You're right. I am a hopeless romantic. Maybe someday it will pay off."

"You mean it, don't you?" she whispered, that blank facade coming down, along with the fragile one I recognized. Underneath she was...raw. Beautiful. "You wouldn't hurt anyone by cheating or abuse."

I shook my head, unlocking my jaw painfully. "Fucking never."

A sound rose in her throat and in that second I knew exactly what happened to give her this fractured view of the world. She whirled on her heel, darting for the only other place she could run to hide in—the bathroom.

"You wanna know what a good man looks like, Skye?" I caught her swiftly and turned her into the circle of my arms, drawing her to my chest. "A good man protects. A good man knows when the boundaries have been crossed." I released her, watching her lips part as furious breaths panted past them. "But despite that, a good man will stay."

Stepping back, I kept an eye on her, ready to catch her if she—hell, after that I wasn't ready to say she might swoon but...yeah.

Swoon would fit.

CHAPTER THREE

HUDSON

"Filter, remember?" she murmured, her breaths slowing. "Why do you have to be so damn perfect?" Her sigh was long, hard, and heartfelt.

My chest ached for her. "I'm far from perfect, Skye. But I'll try to make up for the asshole who carved fear in your heart."

"Humble too, huh?" She shook her head, scraping her hands through her hair and pushing it back off her face. "Maybe you should be the ones writing the articles."

"That'd be a fun column." I smirked. "The world

according to Hudson. Yeah, I can see that being used as toilet paper."

Her smile softened. "You have no idea how powerful those words were to hear, do you?"

"Just a California boy on a beach trip." I shrugged, rubbing the back of my neck.

Her lilies and dewdrops scent wafted around me, filling my head with images of lazy afternoons in the cottage, kissing her until our mouths were puffy with it, and feeding her. That was a different fantasy all on its own. Fuck, just being near her was intoxicating. I couldn't imagine being this close to her full time. I'd never get an inch of work done, she was that damn distracting.

"Is that all?" She bit her lip, closing the distance between us, her lashes fluttering as she looked up at me and away a little too fast.

I caught her chin in my fingers, gently directing her gaze back to meet mine. "Yeah." My mouth dried on the lie. The partial lie. *I have to get fucking past this.* "I'm not that deep, beach girl. Just a guy having downtime."

"And what about the shady as fuck little shop you disappeared into yesterday? You came out smelling like pot and...other stale substances." Her nose wrinkled.

I barked a sharp laugh. "Gonna dig into all my secrets, princess?" I backed her into the wall, bracing my hands either side of her head, my arms at full extension to keep some semblance of distance, even if it was a shitty facade.

"Maybe?" She had the balls to toss her hair. Silky strands wrapped around my forearms, slithering over my skin like she'd just run her fingers along me.

I found it damn hard to breathe.

"Then dig, but don't be shocked when I wanna do a little exposing of my own." I dropped a hand to trace her ribs, resting my knuckles lightly against the sweet curve of her hip. If I wrapped my hand around her, she'd be wearing nothing in a short period and I wasn't about to break my promise to her–I wouldn't force her or put her on the spot so bad she felt like she had to choose something she didn't want.

Yeah, I was that kind of soppy romantic ass.

I shouldn't have worried.

Her hands pressed to my abs in answer, sliding up–thankfully, as my grasp on my control frayed–to rest on my chest. "Who are you, Hudson Whittington?" she breathed.

"Just a guy..." I leaned down and pressed my mouth over hers.

So much for resolve. Or not getting involved.

Fuck it. I need to taste her.

Her lips parted on a gasp as if she wasn't sure I'd take it that far and actually kiss her. I brushed my tongue across the gap between her lips, touching to hers, and I was fucked. All over.

Threading my hands through her gloriously soft hair, I plunged my tongue into her mouth in a dominating dance to glide along hers. A soft, throaty noise whispered between us, and suddenly mine weren't the only hands wandering.

Her nails scraped my shoulders lightly, and she tugged my hair, opening to me fully. I groaned into her mouth, running my palms the length of her body and cupping her ass to tuck her into me. She fit perfectly against me in every way. My knuckles grazed the wall, righting my sense of geography that skewed as I sank against her, grinding her body with mine. The soft little sounds she elicited riled me until we were a mess of roaming hands and wet mouths exploring each other.

Two days of teasing was enough to break both of us, apparently.

Swinging her up onto my hips, I tucked her ankles around me and backed up to the bed. The mattress butted the back of my knees, and I let us fall, with her on top.

Skye's squeak did the best things to my body. I pushed her down onto my erection, rubbing her bikini clad pussy over my length until I swore I'd burst in my pants. When she broke the kiss, slithering down my body to mouth my cock through my shorts, I nearly did.

Tangling my hands in her hair, I let her play, teasing me through the material with her tongue while figuring out how to free my cock with her hands while her mouth was busy. I breathed through my nose hard, levering up to watch her play as she managed to expose my skin to the warm Tijuana air, and lapped at my cock.

"Fuck, Skye," I whispered, fisting her hair gently, and let her have control.

"Yes, please." She gave me an impish grin that shot pure lust through my veins.

Her mouth did wonderful things, teasing and torturing me until I had to pull her up my body or paint her face with my name.

"Come up to me, princess. Right here." I patted my chest as she kneeled over me, her sapphire eyes glowing. Playing with the strings on her bikini, I traced my fingers along her covered skin like she'd teased me until a little wet spot formed and her breaths came too fast. "Nu uh. I want that cream in my mouth." I tucked my hands around the backs of her thighs and drew her over my face.

"Are you sure," she whispered, staring down at me.

"I'll never lie to you, Skye." *Except about who I am. Fuck.* That twinged, but I managed to keep my resistance off my face. I hoped. "Hands here." Capturing her wrists in a gentle hold, I guided them over my head to the bed frame, linking her fingers around the cool metal bar. "Don't let go until I spank this perfect ass. You got it?"

"Got it," she breathed, her hair tumbling over her face to almost hide her eyes that took in *everything*.

When was the last time this girl was loved, for fuck's sake? She was due for more than a little TLC. I got that her sharp edges and hard outlook might scare off a lesser man, but fuck it. That was his loss.

Cupping her ass I went to town, licking her sweetly, nipping and sucking until I learned the rhythm that did it for her, and which spots earned me the best sounds. Her thighs trembled around my head, and I knew I'd never forget the vision of her head flung back, screaming her orgasm as she came on my face.

Or the sweet, addictive taste of her.

No way in hell did I want to let this girl go, lies and work be damned.

Her legs trembled as I dived back in, managing to time my spanks with the crest of her second wave. Skye slumped forward, moaning over me. I tipped her gently sideways, angling her to slide along my body, both of us covered with a sheen of sweat and salt that allowed her to slither along my chest.

"Baby. Skye," I murmured, kissing her gently as she fell bonelessly into my arms, rolling on top of her body. "I need a condom if you have one." If she didn't...shit. It'd be a ten second nudie dash back to my own room while I prayed she hadn't changed her mind.

"Huh?" She blinked at me dozily, so cute and flushed I kissed her again and again until our bodies ground together in a slow rhythm designed to last hours.

"Condom, princess. Or I'll get something." I half rose on my elbows, but she pulled me back.

"Don't go anywhere," she murmured in that breathy voice that drove me crazy. "In my bag. That one. Blue. That– yes. Pocket." She managed one word guidance as I scrounged and found the crinkled foil that made me a happy man.

I ripped the pack open and rolled the condom

on, playing with her creamy pussy with my other hand. "Ready enough for me, princess?"

Her fingers grazed my length, and she spread her legs wide, hooking one knee over my hip and pushing her heel into my ass, driving me forward. "God, yes," she sighed.

Her head tipped back as I rubbed against her, then notched at her entrance, pushing inside. Heat enveloped me in a tight ring, leaving me breathing hard.

"Fuck, you're tight." I groaned, hanging my head down as she wiggled around me.

"Deeper," she demanded.

I slammed a hand to her hip, inching my way inside her, but unable to control myself with that sort of pretty little ass wiggle going on.

Skye gasped, her eyes flaring wide. "You said..."

"I said a lot of things, princess, and I can make love like any man, but I've also wanted to fuck you since you first threw your towel down next to mine on the beach." I slammed home, her cry and the way she strangled my cock with her pretty slicked pussy rocking me deeper, just like she begged. "Wish granted." I bottomed out, stroking her hair back from her face as I stilled. "You okay, Skye?" I pulled her out of her reverie somewhat.

"Yeah," she whispered, shuddering a little. "Go slow and– and deep for a second." Her eyelashes fluttered, mirroring the way she clamped down on me.

My instinct was to screw her hard and fast, but the girl knew what she wanted, and I was only starting to learn what she needed. Rocking deeper into her, I cupped the back of her head, holding our mouths together so we shared each frantic breath, pushing deeper into her like she asked.

Maybe a little rougher.

Her hands gripping my shoulders, she leveraged herself against me, meeting every thrust, both legs wrapped around me. Her first cry lit my soul on fire as she fucked herself on me, and when she faltered, I took over, driving deeper and not stopping, not even when she cried out, shivering in my arms. Damp strands clung to her face. I swept them out of the way so I could lick her throat, sucking and nibbling.

"Perfect, so fucking perfect." I soothed her with gentle kisses, slowing a little as she gazed up at me like I was nothing she'd ever seen before. "Don't let anyone ever tell you otherwise."

I kissed her long and slow, matching my thrusts to the rhythm we set together, showing her what beach love should feel like.

Skye came for me twice more before my spine tingled, signaling the end of my front row seat to watch her shatter around me again and again.

"So beautiful," I murmured, kissing her as I drove into her harder.

Skye's body tensed, and, already recognizing her reaction, I dug my fingers into her ass cheeks and slammed myself home, bellowing my release that mingled with hers.

I dropped my head to her shoulder and gathered her into my arms, the ocean lapping the shore outside the only sound that intruded on our peace.

CHAPTER FOUR

HUDSON

"It looks good." I tallied up the collection of baggies in my possession filled with thousands of dollars of street value and held out my hand. "Be back next month."

Tag shook greasily, and I wished I hadn't extended the favor.

"You'll be back faster than that," Angel huffed from his accounting pile. "Shit sells faster than fresh buds."

"Whatever." I breathed slow, controlled, and hopefully not too deep. *Nearly done.*

All that was left was to head back to Texas without being arrested, though I got the impression from Archer that the badge in my glove compartment would cover my ass back across the border.

That was all I had to achieve... that, and say goodbye to Skye.

I left her in her bed before I crawled back to my room and changed, trying to get my head around the job and out of her pussy. Because that's where my mouth had been when I realized I needed to move my ass. Waiting for her orgasm to crest, I licked her soothingly, tonging her swollen pussy lips from our frantic fuck sessions the night before.

Neither of us got much sleep, and I didn't relish pulling an all nighter in time to haul my ass in front of Archer first thing tomorrow. I wouldn't look fresh, but that was another thing I got about him. In this sort of job I didn't need to be, at least not first thing or the job I was sent to do wasn't done right.

"Thanks, man," I said to no one, tucking the baggies into my jeans and shooting a wave over my shoulder.

No one objected to my leaving, so I figured Agel would probably pocket the extra two hundred in the stacks later without telling his boss of the little bonus.

It was good to have a man in your pocket on the

other side, especially when part of me wondered that I wouldn't be sent back across the border if I earned that badge the way I hoped.

I slipped back into my room and found Skye sitting on my bed. "What are you doing in here?" My words came out harsh and I winced. "Sorry, I was..."

"Doing man shit. I remember." She looked at me through a curtain of glossy blonde waves. "And I remember falling asleep after you made me come, and eating my breakfast alone." She pouted, taking the sting out of her words.

I exhaled through my nose. "Yeah. Sorry about that." I headed for my luggage and knew there was no way she wasn't going to see the drugs I had to take back to fulfill my agreement with Archer. To prove my worth.

Shit.

"You wanna go get something else? Coffees? My treat." I offered, pulling cash out of my pocket.

She eyed the wad and shook her head. "Nope. I'm all packed and ready to go. Just gotta find a bus that suits my timetable."

"Where you headed?"

I never asked. I never thought I'd want to know. Kneeling, I pulled my luggage apart and ran my hand along the inner compartment. Maybe if I could get her to grab stuff from my bathroom...

"Texas. Austin."

A stupid ass grin spread over my face. "You don't say." I rolled my lips and made a decision. A shit one, but I had to play this out somehow. "Want a lift?"

"That's a long drive." She eyed me as I drew the drugs out of my pocket and lined the inner compartment with them. "I knew that's what you were doing," she said quietly.

"Yeah? Did it scare you?" My heart thumped traitorously in my chest.

"Nope."

"You say that a lot." I zipped the pouch and rocked back on my heels. "Want a ride in my noisy old truck instead of a communal public bus?"

She wrinkled her nose. "Hell, yes. You know, I thought you were from California."

"What makes you say that?" I kept my tone light though my shoulders tightened.

"Dunno." She shrugged and tossed her hair. "You seem like California. Sunshine and shit. I'll get my stuff. Don't you run off on me, baby oil boy," she warned.

A dopey ass grin left my cheeks aching, right up

until I had her strapped into my truck and turned over the engine that thankfully behaved itself. In fact, the grin lasted until we were several hours into the drive and she opened her laptop. Then a few things hit home real damn hard.

"Is this a fling where we go our separate ways at the other end?" I said quietly.

Skye swallowed. "Is this because I write articles you hate?" She peered at me through her lashes, and my dick swelled.

I shifted uncomfortably in my seat. "I don't wanna say goodbye to you, princess." My knuckles glowed white against the worn leather of my steering wheel.

"I don't want that either." She nibbled her lip.

I waited, but that seemed to be all she would say. My eyes squeezed tight, and I slapped my hand on the steering wheel. "Fuck it. Lying shits me and I made you a promise I don't want to break. I'm working with the Texas Ranger unit in Austin. I love what we have going, and screw it if that's the hope-less, soppy romantic in me coming out. But I don't want you thinking I'm some damn drug dealer. And...you're right. I was in California. As a fire-fighter in LA." I slammed my mouth shut, grinding my teeth. I didn't care if I just screwed myself seven ways to Sunday. She was worth it.

Skye mulled on that for a few miles. "So, you're a Texas Ranger, huh?" She twined her hands in her lap. "It was easier to believe you were a boy who loved fun and sun."

I raked my fingers through my hair. "I am. Usually. This was my first...job, or whatever. Kinda like an audition. If I fucked it up, then I don't get to stay, and I'll be going back to Cali. If I didn't screw it up, then I call Cali and I'm gonna make my boss real unhappy."

"You're good at your job?" She played with the hem of her pink cotton skirt with gold tassels.

"I have a lot of years in that job, and I know it well," I replied, trying to take my ego out of it.

"Sounds like you have a home there."

I breathed out. "Yeah, change is scary. But this offer came through and...I like the idea of being able to help. I don't know. That's stupid."

"It's not," she said in the same quiet tone I used with her before. A strange echo, but I got it. Kinda part of the snarky-fuck-frenzy-reflective vibe thing we had going on. "I think you'll suit it either way."

I slid my gaze across to her. "You know many Texas Rangers, Skye?"

She shrugged. "I've seen them getting medals, read about them in the paper. I live in Austin. It's impossible not to know about them."

"Fair enough." I swallowed and held out my arm.

She made a soft sound that kickstarted my heart, scooting across the bench and snuggling into my side. Her hand rested on my chest, her cheek on my shoulder. "You feel good."

"Yeah?" I kissed the top of her head. "So, we gonna try this thing when we get–" I cut that sentence off.

There was no guarantee I had the job. Hell, I already broke one of the cardinal rules, and we just left Mexico.

"I wanna try." She looked up at me and I swore I could fall into those blue eyes of hers and never come out. "No matter what happens. I can travel and stuff." She went back to studying her skirt.

My heart clenched. If I didn't get the job, I'd be back in LA and a firefighter didn't get the luxury or freedom of travel, or that many days off. Pulling overtime had been my life for the last few years, and I wasn't sure I could sit still for longer than a week on a beach.

"Whatever happens," I echoed, resting my cheek on her hair and tugging her closer. "Fuck it." I pulled over, throwing the truck into neutral and tipped her chin up.

"What—" Skye's protest died as I claimed her mouth, pushing her down onto the bench seat and kissed the hell out of both of us.

CHAPTER FIVE

HUDSON

I left Skye in my truck, unwilling to drop her off until I could tell her what sort of future I had. I couldn't think much beyond that while I stuffed the drugs into my jacket pockets, and kissed her thoroughly.

"You'll be great," she whispered, curling her fingers around my collar and pulling me down for one more kiss. "I have faith in you."

I was glad one of us did.

My jaw aching, I sucked in the vision of her perched on the bench seat, her tasseled gold and pink skirt fluttering around her stunning legs, a filmy floral blouse I nearly ripped open early in the trip in a need to be closer to her a soft contrast to her tan and the golden waves draped around her.

I walked into the Austin unit's headquarters in my jeans, boots and a t-shirt, not having shaved and looking exactly as I should for a twenty something hour drive with rest stops where I spent my time not looking at the road and my hand buried in Skye's pussy.

But now wasn't the time to think about that.

The office was empty except for Archer's closed door when I made it up the stairs, doing the deep breathing thing and probably sounding like a rampaging bull.

"Come in," Archer answered my knock.

I pushed the door open to the sparsest office I'd ever seen. My second time in it and the empty space still got me. A neat row of filing cabinets lined one wall, and a scarred wooden desk took up the space opposite the door, a single chair either side.

One was occupied by a man with red-brown longish hair, wearing a blue checked shirt, a worn leather ledger open on his desk that he closed as I entered.

"That looks like it gets about as much love as my steering wheel," I greeted him, pulling out the packets of drugs from my pockets and lining them up neatly by type on his desk, along with a list on my phone, including a description of everything I saw in Tijuana.

"Must love that truck then, Hudson. Good work," Archer said as I reached into my back pocket and pulled out the badge, placing it carefully before him and stepping back. "What's this?"

"It's yours." I kept my shoulders straight and stepped back.

I told Skye the truth. I wouldn't lie, not if I didn't have to.

"Is it?" Archer picked up the polished metal. "You know the history of these? They used to be made from Mexican pesos, a five and eight. Today, Rangers get two. One like this to carry day to day, and this sort." He pulled open a desk drawer and flicked a shiny metal badge my way.

I caught it one-handed and studied the coin set into a star. "It's solid history."

"It is." Archer shook his head when I extended my hand. "That's yours, Hudson."

I swallowed hard. "I broke your rules."

"Did you?" His gaze was unfathomable, but he made no move to take the badge from me. I placed it next to the other one on his desk and stepped back. "How?"

"I told a girl about the job. She came back with

me, and I hated lying to her, letting her think I ran drugs."

Archer nodded, his mouth opening. A rap from behind me nearly jerked me out of my skin. Archer didn't smile, though something flickered in his eyes.

"Come in."

The door opened and a tall woman in caramel pants and a white shirt entered the office. Her blonde hair was scraped back in a tight knot at the back of her neck. She held a white hat in her hands and stopped stiffly beside me.

If it wasn't for her blue eyes I might not have believed what I was seeing.

"Sir," Skye said in a hard voice.

I had nothing left. Everything we'd done...My stomach curled, and I breathed in hard. "Thank you for the experience, Archer. I'll leave you to it." I nodded respectfully, though Skye wouldn't even look at me, and made it as far as the door before Archer stopped me.

"Ranger." His voice sliced through the air, and even though I wasn't sure he was talking to me, I turned back. "Get your ass back here, Hudson. I'm not done."

"Sir." I reclaimed my spot on the worn carpet

beneath my feet, my movements as jerky as Skye's, who hadn't moved since she entered the room.

"Report." Archer watched me unblinkingly but spoke to Skye.

"The job was well executed. He might be a little unorthodox, but his methods worked well enough."

I tried not to grind my teeth and failed.

"Anything else?" Archer asked, leaning back in his chair.

"He broke cover on the way back." She didn't so much as look at me.

I swore my heart shattered right there and then.

"You weren't meant to travel together." Archer raised his eyebrows. "You changed the rules."

A tiny petal of hope painted in pinks and golds unfurled in my chest.

"Yes, sir." Skye stood rigid, her hands clasped behind her back, the knuckles white, the only outward expression of her tension. And like her face when I burst into her room in Tijuana, she was blank. Almost unreadable.

Except maybe to Archer. That man could be faced with a brick wall and deduce something from it. I'd put a full month's pay on that bet.

"Recommendation?"

She paused for a full minute while my heart

stalled with her. "He would be a solid asset if his morals don't trip him up."

Archer faced me in full, leaning forward. "Skye Hamilton was part of an older unit recently disbanded. She isn't used to how we run things here," –the corner of his mouth twitched, I swore– "but she's getting used to it. She also needs a partner." He collected both badges in his palm and held them out. "Job's yours, Hudson."

I swallowed. "I broke your rules." I seemed to be stuck on that.

"She changed them."

"We're good?"

"We are." Archer nodded, turning his attention to Skye. "Will working with Hudson be a problem?"

She breathed out hard through tight lips, her cheeks two spots of colour. "Not at all, sir."

"Good. He's your partner. There's a file on your desks. Dismissed." Archer opened his ledger and dropped his head.

And just like that I was a fully-fledged Texas Ranger.

I reached back, opening the door to his office. "After you," I murmured, the motion automatic.

The glare in her eyes wasn't.

Still frantic and untrusting.

Looked like I had a hell of a time before me to rebuild that with her. Because there was no chance I was letting her go.

"I knew those articles couldn't be real," I murmured as she passed me.

"They are fucking real, Hudson," she gritted out. "I've been writing them for years." Skye powered through the door, leaving me huffing a laugh in her wake.

"Hudson."

"Sir?" I pivoted sharply on my heel.

"Careful with her. She's had an abusive history. Not my story to tell."

Smiling faintly, I stepped into the doorway. "I know."

Archer nodded, the hint of a matching smile lighting his face as I pulled the office door shut.

I made it a good four steps to my desk, the one with my name on a damn engraved triangular thing, before Skye accosted me.

"You don't touch me, or kiss me, or–"

I ignored her outburst, and the new set of rules she tossed in my face and clasped her shoulders gently. "You got your say last time when you claimed me as your beach bodyguard. No, I don't care under what conditions." I pressed a finger over her lips.

"Here's my rules. Tell me everything. Don't hide shit from me. My side of that is I'll always have your back, no matter what. But I want to give this thing a go, Skye. I want to see if we can make it work."

"But what happened in Ti–"

"Was fucking amazing," I said softly, tucking a stray piece of gold hair behind her ear. "And for the record, this Skye is just as sexy as gold tasseled Skye and Bikini Skye."

"Objectifying," she muttered, her color heightening as she looked at me through her lashes.

"You bet your perfect fucking behind." I leaned in slowly, giving her time to pull away and kissed the corner of her mouth. "Gonna try this with me?"

She turned enough for me to capture her mouth in full. When I kissed her a little harder she didn't push me away, opening her lips and letting me in.

"Fine." She pulled back, and gave me sassy eyes. I couldn't wait to see what my handprint looked like on her ass. "Can we get to work now, Big Boy?"

"Keep it up, Skye. I'm keeping count." I slammed my hand down on my thigh, the crack reverberating around the room.

She held my gaze and raised her chin. "Do your worst, Hudson."

A grin spread over my face as I grabbed the file

and started flicking through, my mind already headed in other directions. "Oh, I plan to. Hell girl, I might even be able to show you what real love looks like."

Her eyes widened to the point of comical, and I pulled her to me for another heartfelt kiss, putting everything I was right behind that not-so-simple touch of lips on lips.

"You can't be serious," she whispered. "It's been a week."

I shrugged. *Fuck it.* What did I have to lose? Nothing but a stunning girl who happened to be my partner both day and night. "I'm all in, Skye. All for you."

"Romantic ass."

I huffed a laugh and tweaked her nose just to earn a glare.

Having Skye as both partner and girlfriend would be one hell of a challenge, but damn would I enjoy showing her all the ways a man could be romantic with a demanding woman he'd already fallen for, however long our partnership lasted.

Maybe for a long while.

Maybe forever.

There was no better way to test it than a road trip to South Carolina.

CHAPTER FIVE

SKYE

Hudson Whittingdon was a royal ass.

A sexy ass, an objectifying ass, and my brand spanking new partner.

Shit. Archer really pulled the wool over my eyes with that one and I was far from proud of it. Not that he seemed fazed that I slept with the newb, even though it horrified me more than a little bit. I assumed I'd be able to sweep the whole situation away as a summer fling in undercover work. That shit happened all the time. Then I'd transfer to another unit and the intimate skin-on-skin moments we shared would become stuff of urban legend.

Instead, my fling was my partner, confessing all

sorts of flowery bullshit I didn't believe in and now we were headed to...

Ba da ba boom–

A place called Love Beach. Hello, South Carolina. Where we were supposed to be newly-weds and keep an eye on a target that should never be part of our scope.

On the dash sat the plain gold band I was supposed to wear but couldn't bring myself to face the confining feeling, even if it was fake as fuck.

Hudson, the show off, put his on hours ago before we headed into Love Beach after our road trip.

No fucking lie. That's what the place was called, and we were headed there right now, with a fresh change of panties in a packed truck. The manilla folder sat in my lap and I once again sat gunshot in Hudson's truck heading into the stupidly-named town in South Carolina.

Instead of trying to even things with Hudson, or deal with the way he kissed me back in the office, I opted to ignore the huge beefy Ranger in the driver's seat and chose instead to study the small town's main street. Not overpopulated, it was still obvious which of those wandering along the row of shops and service providers was a local and which were the tourists purely by their dress.

The locals were much more laid back, and the travelers donned enormous floppy hats as their weapon of choice that had the locals dodging back on more than one occasion as they shared a sidewalk together.

The shops looked clean, if brightly colored, as if a family or PG rated movie vomited all over the place. And here we were, supposed to watch for a smuggler who escaped Texas Rangers on their own turf, study the target's habits, and bring back all our observations without doing a single thing to apprehend the man who took three lives on Texas land not a month before.

Was I impressed?

No ma'am, I was not.

Apparently, Archer hadn't got his ass in gear enough to get the man himself, but Hudson was as gung ho with this little test as he had been in Tijuana.

I wondered if his tastes in women and relationships fluctuated as fast as his attention. I rather suspected they did and I was simply a fast and furious summer passion in a long line of fling-like conquests reaching from California to Texas, no matter what he said back in the office, or any day since.

He kept insisting we were fine and it wasn't a week long thing.

Fine, two weeks, then.

The blur of color along the main street melded into a rainbow of pastels, and as soon as I noted the ice cream parlor on one end of a block, my stomach rumbled.

Hudson laughed, his deep voice reverberating around the cab in a far too appealing sound.

"Don't do that," I snapped.

"Do what?" He affected a wounded look, all puppy dog eyes, downturned mouth and wrinkly forehead.

I slapped the arm he slid across my shoulders, pushing him back. I sighed. The man was relentless, and not in a good way. Or maybe I did like his ways, and just hated that about myself, too.

I had a whole lot of hate for a stack of things right now.

I spotted something I didn't hate and threw out a hand, slapping the passenger window with my knuckles. "Stop here."

Hudson slammed on the brakes, eliciting a stream of honks behind us and dived into a space way too small for his monster of a vehicle. "This good?"

I pried open a squinted eye. "Do I need to order a funeral service for any small animals or grannies?"

"Hey, that's not nice. And you never know. Grannies in Texas be badass." He smirked.

I nodded at his nonsense and hauled my ass out of the truck. "Stay."

His laugh followed me as he bounded to the sideway and fell into step at my side. "Not a dog, Skye."

"But you're still my bitch." The barb was hollow and meaningless. A wave of tiredness hit me. "Where are we staying?"

"I mean, I'm happy to be your bitch but my girl's gotta tell me what's up, otherwise I can't take care of her. 'Kay?" He nuzzled my temple.

I batted him away before I could catch something, like feelings.

Already did that.

I ignored my annoying voices, too.

"We're working. We don't have time for things like this." I lifted my pace.

Hudson matched me step for step. "You're hell bent on this investigation, huh?" The back of his hand brushed mine and I repressed the shiver that raced through my body and along my arms, turning into Caffeine Beach, the coffee shop I spotted earlier.

"I'm hell bent on getting this done, going home and starting real work," I snapped back. "Not going to apologize, because this is a bullshit assignment, much like the last."

"Aw, Archer wouldn't do that to us. He needs this information." Hudson caught my hand this time, linking our fingers together. His were thicker and speared my fingers apart. I hated that I liked the feeling that he was bigger than me. Could actually take everything I threw at him.

Not appropriate on the job.

Besides, I knew a few things about his precious Archer that he clearly didn't.

Like that the man wasn't invested in the unit and was closing up shop, handing the unit over to the next most capable man, and heading north. Real far north, like Montana. Borderlands area. About as far as a person could get without actually needing a passport.

But I didn't say any of that because a large part of me knew I would need it for a rainy day sometime. Maybe soon.

I yanked my hand free. "You don't call having no arrest at the end of the assignment progress?" I walked straight up to the counter. "Giant long black please, four shots, no sugar. Thanks." The waitress looked at me doubtfully, but wrote down my order without any more questions, thankfully.

"Well we are on this one, so why don't you start behaving less like a cop and more like the girl I'm supposed to have just married?" Hudson whispered in my ear, flicking his tongue along the curve in a way that liquefied and overheated all of my internal functions.

I shivered lightly against him, and made to push him back but the smart ass expected the move and caught my wrists, twirling me expertly in his arms. The moment my mouth opened to protest, he covered it with his in a seriously pornographic kiss that would have ended in bed had we been in an enclosed space. Instead, my red face flamed along with probably anyone else in the shop who couldn't possibly avoid the PDA he put on.

"Aren't you overdoing it?" I whispered, looking coyly up at him through my lashes, fluttering them and stepping on his toes to let him know he crossed a line.

The big boof didn't buy into my play. His expression grew serious, and it stalled me, the way he looked at me, all intense and complicated.

Life needs to be simple. In and out. Hi and bye.

I couldn't do complicated any more, not now or ever. Never again.

I couldn't.

The corners of Hudson's lips turned up in the sort of sexy smile that left me leaning into him whether my brain screamed at me to retain my independence, or not.

"Aw, come on, Skye. I just found you. Don't ruin my day." His fingers knotted around my hand as his mouth lowered over mine, leaving just enough space for a single breath before he kissed me again.

A dare to defy him in public.

Spoilers: I didn't.

His tongue dragged over mine, his pace slow, but dominating, a reminder of the way he fucked me by the beach in Mexico. A moan caught in my throat before I remembered where we were.

When he pulled back, he wore a satisfied smirk and a gold band sat on my left ring finger.

Asshole.

CHAPTER SIX

HUDSON

Skye bamboozled me at every turn. Back on the beach she could have been an ice queen, for fuck's sake. In Texas, I got to see the hard ass side that appealed to Archer enough that he hired her.

Here in South Carolina? She ran hot as Hades, but sure as hell it wasn't at me.

Because that ring on her finger scared the daylights outta her, and everyone around us could see her fear right there on display.

My stomach cramped. I slung an arm around her, pulling her into my chest. "Easy, honey," I murmured.

Fuck, this assignment will be blown before we

touch foot in our apartment. A joint holiday—ahem, honeymoon—apartment with one bed, ostensibly.

Guess I'm sleeping on the sofa.

"Don't *honey* me," she snapped, but thankfully my shirt muffled the sound and only I heard it. Maybe.

An older couple eyed us, and I gave them what I hoped was a Californian winning grin. What a way to do fifty states in five minutes. The girl sent my head on a whirlwind tour of my own sanity. How the hell we were supposed to be partners in this thing while all I wanted to do was find a quiet space and fuck like bunnies for the next hour eluded me.

Her, too, from the dazed look in her eyes.

Huh. I liked that one.

"Don't do that," she murmured, a little softer, thankfully.

"All part of the show." I affected a swagger I sure as hell didn't feel with her looking at me with a decent dollop of distrust as she swiped her fingers—glittering with that ring—over her pink mouth I just wanted to kiss some more.

Because she tasted like sunshine and sand and new beginnings and I never wanted to stop.

"We have a job to do," she reminded me, one

hand still curled in my shirt from our PDA. She looked down at it, surprise written across her stunning features, and pried her fingers free, flexing them.

"Way to give a guy a boner and whiplash in one. This is the assignment, *honey*," I said pointedly.

"What, being a demanding asshole?" She pivoted in the circle of my arms, and stared around. "Ah, there's a good place to start." She strode forward, or tried to, but I pulled her back.

"Teamwork. There's no I in it, Skye."

"Exactly. So we do this my way."

"Or we find our accommodation and get it done the Archer way."

Her laugh tinkled around me like silver bells before her voice sliced through the effect laced heavily with derision. "There's brown on your nose, Ranger. Did you know?" Her hair flicked me in the face as she marched forward.

I caught her hand, catching up with her all too easily, and fast enough I noted the tight expression on her face before she managed to hide it.

Ahh. That explained a lot. Perhaps our cover story was a little too good.

"You can be the Ranger if you want," I said

softly. "I'll be satisfied with being the house husband."

Her brow dipped though she didn't look at me. "I don't think anyone would buy that."

"And yet here you are." I squeezed her hand. "Busting past all the odds and expectations of failure."

She stopped short. "What did you say?"

I caught her chin. "What aren't you saying, princess?" She said nothing and I smiled slightly. "Hit a nerve, huh?"

Her gaze drifted past me and before I could snark at her further, her expression cleared and she pulled her hand from mine.

"Stay here, househusband."

"Is this how it's always going to be?" I called to her sexy backside that disappeared inside a jewelry shop.

"Better catch her now. Not a good habit to get into already." The older gent and his wife winked at me.

I managed a smile and followed Skye toward the shop she disappeared into, nearly face planting right into her as she busted back on out.

"Whoa. That was fast. Didn't find what you wanted?" I asked carefully.

Skye beamed at me. "Nope. Got exactly what I wanted."

I waited for more but there was nothing forthcoming.

"Hope it was his credit card, love." The matching lady with the older gent called gaily, waving a bag that looked cute and colorful, and probably cost a month's wage.

Skye laughed, nope. Not laughed. Giggled. My girl *giggled*. The sound stunned me for a moment before I pulled my shit together and slipped my arms around her waist.

She didn't so much as flinch, leaning into me and rising up onto her toes right there in the doorway to the jewelry shop.

"I found our mark-co," she sang softly, shuffling her feet to let the next customer out.

The guy stood at least as tall as me and looked like something from the Godfather—or maybe the rap sheet in the manilla folder that Skye cuddled the entire way to South Carolina.

Tall, dark and broody looking, the dude looked like he could scent a bad deal or a weak chin a mile away. Or maybe a fake pair of tits.

Because right now my mark had eyes for one person.

Skye.

His gaze dropped down her body like he planned on undressing her. She giggled again, shimmying against me and more than one thing rose to attention.

Fortunately, it was my temper that cooled first as I hauled her against me and out of his way.

"This way, Skye. Let the gentleman pass," I forced out pleasantly through gritted teeth.

"Not a problem at all." He placed a hand on Skye's shoulder and trailed his finger along her arm. "Is it, darlin'?"

She fucking well *sighed* into me.

The hell?

"Not at all, Marco. This is my husband, Hudson. Say hi to the nice man, Huddy," she giggled again.

That noise was starting to get to me.

"Hi," I said politely when my brain froze on the image of spanking the sound right out of her. From the look on Marco's face, I wasn't alone in my assessment of her behavior. "Do you to know each other?"

"Oh no," Said Skye, her face pink with the half-truth.

"Yes," said Marco, looking me straight in the eye and offering a smirk. "Marcus Torrino. Or Marco." He shrugged.

Got yourself a gangland name there, Mister Marco Torrino?

Either name would flag with Interpol and a dozen smaller home-based units, including ours. Archer took me through the process, and Brodie after on a fast call to bring me up to date. What I couldn't work out was how Miss Skye made a new friend in thirty seconds or less in a shop.

"Oh, Marco reads my blog." Skye looked up at me, her eyes shining, and blushed.

"Ah." My brain blanked totally. No wonder she looked so damn happy, especially after I tore her apart for her opinions. "And, uh, what do you think?"

God, I hoped my profile said I was meant to be stupid, because I fucking well sounded like it.

"Yes, he loved the one about empowering women. You remember the one you read on the beach?" Her smile remained, though her eyes turned hard.

"Yes." I broke her gaze and grinned at Marco. "She loves pulling a guy apart."

"Indeed." His eyes never left her. "I have a party on my yacht tonight. At Passion Cove. The *Serenade.* Would you like to attend?" His gaze lifted and his smirk that she seemed to eat right up remained.

"Both of you, of course. I'm sure I can find something for you to do while I entertain your...wife."

Fuck me if the leech wasn't hitting on her right in front of me and telling me he'd fuck her while I drank his boat dry.

It's an assignment.

She's a summer fling.

And summer felt like it was already nearly over. Maybe a little too fast for my liking.

The truth was that I didn't want this thing with her to end, though it likely had to if we were to remain partners and not end up hating each other. I foresaw a whole lot of nights alone in my new place in Texas with my hand as company while she partied hard on yachts with this crook.

Cover job or not, I wasn't ready to let her sell herself just for a case that, like she said, was going nowhere. But it might in future. I knew the Ranger unit worked to feed information to various police precincts on different cases and helped out as an umbrella to pass down information.

On the other hand I understood the need to close up a test case like this as fast as possible and earn a few hat feathers like Skye wanted.

It just wasn't going to be on this job. And I didn't

have to like another man touching her, cover story be damned.

"I'm sure we can make time. After we find our accommodation and...break it in," I said baldly, squeezing Skye until she squeaked and shot me a sexy as hell death stare.

"Definitely." She ignored me pointedly when I kissed along her shoulder, overplaying the enamored honeymooner. She dug her blunt nails into the back of my hands until I was certain they would bear little crescent moons in perpetuity. "What time tonight, Marco?"

The smile she gave him was nothing like the tight ones she offered me the entire trip.

"Shall we say nine o'clock? Or a little later. I don't mind waiting."

I'm sure you don't, asshole.

"We'll make good use of the time," I promised her, mentally adding a pink peachy ass into that equation.

"We'll see you then," Skye promised.

"Make sure you wear something...nice." He smiled at her, and it turned slimier if such a thing was possible as he glanced at me, amusement lighting his eyes. "Something suitable."

"Can do," I said softly, meeting his gaze and

letting a little of my own fire through the mask I donned the moment we stepped out into the main street of Love Beach.

You wanna play hard, motherfucker? I'll play hard.

"I can't wait," Skye oozed, letting me tow her away before I blew something, like my temper.

Or the case, before it started.

CHAPTER SEVEN

SKYE

I slithered into the dark blue dress after my shower in the main bathroom while Hudson muttered away darkly to himself in the ensuite. The room at Garden House—the entire hotel—was amazing. Everything was color coded. Everything was neat, tidy and looked brand spanking new. The honeymoon suite was more like a presidential suite and I didn't want to know how much the unit shelled out for this little project. Mind, I also didn't know the budget and expectations Archer set, and any new piece of tech could cost more than a week's stay in a place like this.

The bedroom was filled with lace and gold and pinks, with a real fake pink bear rug on the floor, like some sixties or seventies flick regurgitated brand new décor. The effect was fun and flirty, and the amount of details did my head in.

Not that Hudson said much as he towed me inside the room, making sure to kiss me thoroughly on the threshold before pushing me inside with a hard hand that promised naughty things later on.

Naughty things I might or might not crave even if indulging him was a really bad idea.

It seemed smart to get out of his reach until he cooled a little after our chance encounter with our target for the week. Not that I thought getting the required information would take half as much time as Archer expected. My hand brushed the screen of my phone while I contemplated asking for extra duties.

Marco might be a leech, but he was a simple one though dirty in more than the sexual sense, though I knew that was true of him also. Closing up our assignment part B meant heading back to Texas post haste, and maybe going our separate ways. I agreed to partnering with Hudson to get into the unit. Surely it wouldn't be that hard to also extract myself from him.

Hudson showed himself to be possessive, which

meant little freedom, more judginess from Mister McSook, not only too passionate in his...work, but also impractical. Partnering with a constantly green eyed monster was along the lines of my worst nightmare. At the least it meant constantly dealing with possessiveness and the lack of independence which I fought so freaking hard for.

Shaking my hair out, I curled it and left it hanging half down my back, fixing sapphire and diamond earrings to my ears. The dress, one from a different life that Archer suggested might be the sort of attire I'd need on this assignment as though he knew and was still testing us like an overbearing father figure, fit as well as it did the last time I wore it.

I just hoped tonight worked out a whole lot better than last time.

"Skye? I hope you're ready. We need to be there in a bit if we want to scope the place out before we—holy shit." Hudson, as eloquent as ever, halted in the doorway to the main bathroom, his bowtie hanging around his neck and fingers grasping either side like he wasn't sure what to do with it.

I finished with my lipstick and straightened, running my hands along my sides, knowing he'd like it. What? A girl has to get her rocks off somehow and it wouldn't be either of the men who wanted in—or out—of the dress tonight who made me smile next.

"Glad you scrub up well," I murmured, smiling slightly and trying not to drool.

It wasn't only the bowtie that was still undone—I was back to beach bodyguard Hudson, all tan, muscles and tequila nights. So far I'd only seen him in board shorts, or jeans and a tee. Anything else seemed out of uniform for the bulky man. But it wasn't a lie – he did scrub up good. Black pants showed off hard earned thigh muscle, and an expanse of golden skin above the belt line, which was where I fixed my gaze.

On the skin. Above the belt.

Shit, shit, shit.

I glanced up and by the smirk that decorated his drooly face as he surveyed me in kind I knew I'd been busted. His hair was pushed back off his face like a blonde James Bond, all suave and shit.

"Where'd my partner go?" I said without thinking,

"Yeah." He swallowed, his eyes still fixed on me. "Same, honey."

I shook my head, though I wasn't sure if it was at him or me. "If you want the tie done up, then you need to do the shirt up." I clicked my tongue and batted his hands away when he obediently started to button from the bottom up. "No. Never bottom. Start at the top."

"What are you, a reclusive socialite turned Texas Ranger?" he gaped at me as I deftly did his shirt up, avoiding his skin as best I could and made a not so mess of his bow tie.

"There."

"You are a goddess, you know that?" One hand rose to brush over a curl I painstakingly twisted and sprayed until it stayed that way. "And I get to have you."

"Not tonight, sunshine." I batted that hand away too and stepped back, the spell holding us in a sort of charged stasis breaking.

"You wound me," he said softly, not stepping away like I expected, or huffing at me. "He's gonna be trouble tonight. You know that."

I swallowed back the urge to snap but the wounded look on Hudson's face shattered something fragile inside me. Guilt swamped me and I softened my tone. "He's not the only one who'll be trouble." I stepped into him a little. "It's a job, Hudson. Let this thing go."

His brow furrowed. "Why? Because we're partners? If it's because you don't trust me, then seek another Ranger to fuck and dump." The line of his jaw remained hard. He stared at me, his anger turning inward as his body stiffened.

"Maybe it's best." I let out a breath. *That was easier than I expected.*

Then why did I feel so damn shitty about it?

"It's time." Hudson checked his watch, offering no reprieve. "If you get stuck tonight I'll be there, Skye." His voice lowered. "I promise."

I shook my head and gave him an empty smile. "You can't promise me anything at all."

Yep, tonight was going to be just like last time.

I padded across the floor to the door and slipped on my heels that almost brought me to Hudson's height, but not quite. Marco didn't like tall women, and I wondered if I should dumb it down a little more. He seemed to like the bimbo act after all.

"Beautiful," Hudson murmured, right at my elbow. His fingers curled through my arm. "Let's get this show on the road so we can pack the hell up and go home."

We'd only been in the town for a handful of hours and I was more than ready to agree.

If only on that one thing.

The *Serenade* sat moored beside other multimillion dollar yachts on the waterfront. Marco's personal party wasn't the only one in progress. Further along the bay, another boat thumped with music and laughter that carried across the water. Marco's was a small gathering in comparison, but the guest list was that much more exclusive. Without my accidental meeting with the smuggler—whose boat was easily the largest and most expensive in the bay, though I doubted he needed the tax write-off like the software developer's boat we passed earlier, we would never have been able to get on board.

Thank Archer for suggesting we both pack cocktail and black tie attire. It was like he'd known how this assignment would go. Setting aside my instinctive dislike for the man abandoning his unit for a moment, I wondered what else he might expect, and if we would live up to the pedestal he set out for us.

"Behave tonight, and I promise I'll make it worth your while later," Hudson murmured in my ear. His hand slunk around my waist, pulling me back into him. "And I'll let you choose the activity."

"What if I don't pick your favorite thing?" I

asked absently, falling back into our usual, snarky banter.

"But you're my favorite thing." He licked the shell of my ear. "If you fuck him, I'll turn this ass red with one hand and then start with the other."

A shiver rippled over me at the thought, both terrifyingly satisfying and abhorrent in equal measure. "You and your dirty promises."

"Will you take me up on one?" His fingers drifted lower, grazing the front of my dress that didn't feel half the shield that it had been when I first dressed in it. The walk into the cove was wonderful in the way that it cleared my head, but walking next to Hudson when he was brooding.... hurt. In all sorts of ways.

He's not for me.

And yet...he was. Hudson was nothing like the sort of man I usually dated, and I hadn't gone on a date for a long time. Not to say I didn't have one night stands and too many that I was able to forget the first shoddy attempts that got worse by the pick-up. But he offered something I hadn't had—ever.

Security.

I should jump at the opportunity to have someone dote on me but that sort of closeness, the intimacy he needed—that was the terrifying part.

Not his hand on my ass, or me sleeping with someone else. It was the thought that the security he offered might be there one day, and...gone the next.

Cliché, but true.

I'd been there, had it happen, and had to walk away for my own sanity. I sure as hell couldn't do it again.

That was my game. Cement the future of my career. Little to no risk in my personal life, no matter what it took.

But to do that I'd have to break a Ranger's heart.

"Skye, we should have talked—" Hudson started,

"My newest toy." Marco's voice echoed around the boat and the water, gesturing us onto the one hundred million dollar yacht that by rights belonged to someone else, and registered under another man's name, or perhaps another name of Marco's. He had a few, like a collection.

His hands swept out as he said those words, but his gaze remained firmly on me.

Hudson's touch fell away from me, and cold air brushed my back where he stood a moment before, leaving me alone with Marco.

"Don't worry. He's already off doing something he'll find...fun." The corner of Marco's mouth turned up in a dark promise that either meant he expected my new husband to earn himself a night's worth of lap dances from an expensive hooker, or flat his way across the bay come dawn.

It was going to be one of those nights, and I understood this game well.

From the look in Marco's eyes, he expected at least a little better behavior from me than Hudson, and I was more than willing to oblige. For now.

"I'm all yours." I took the hand he extended, my fingers brushing the dark purple silk weave he wore than on a white man might have looked ostentatious but with Marco's Spanish heritage, actually looked quite classy. The open, crisp white shirt beneath spoke of an extra sort of expectation.

"Oh, I know." He leaned down to brush his lips across my ear, erasing Hudson's touch I hated at the time and missed now.

I steeled myself, tipping my chin up and smiling as vapidly as I could. "What game are we playing tonight?" I'd bet my new salary that Marco had something in mind. He always did.

"My favorite game, Miss Skye." He held out his other hand, gesturing me downstairs.

The door shut and the lock flicked before I really heard his words...and the fact I didn't pick him up on it.

Pivoting slowly on my heel I turned to correct his mistake and found myself forehead to barrel with a matte black gun, close enough to read the serial number—if the damn thing hadn't already been filled off.

Double shit.

CHAPTER EIGHT

HUDSON

I didn't make it three steps across the back of the *Serenade* before I knew something was badly wrong.

Sure, Marco was hosting a party—a closed one, with cartel heads openly on the water in front of me. These were men I knew from the flick through of potential guests in Archer's folder that were hot prospects. The hottest sort that rarely showed their faces to an area with CCTV, and certainly not together.

And every single one of them were banded together on the back of the yacht, drinking and making fucking merry.

The only one missing was Marco.

"Cognac, sir?" a server offered politely.

"Thank you." I swallowed my misgivings and selected a cup from the tray he held, inhaling the scent appreciatively, wishing I had Skye by my side to slap some sense into me.

He nodded and moved on, leaning in to speak quietly with the next tuxedoed attendant.

Damnit, everywhere I looked I saw a threat. To her, to everyone in the bay.

We just got here and the whole place looked ready to go right to hell in a heartbeat. I didn't have my girl by my side, no matter how much she fought against the need that linked us both.

Over a week on the beach in Tijuana, a road trip and now this operation...she hadn't slapped me yet, though I was fairly sure she would have if she didn't expect to get herself fired for the effort.

Something told me that Archer wasn't that sort of boss, unless the occasion truly called for it, and it was one of the reasons I crossed state lines to meet him in Texas. Skye's reasons for not trusting him... they were her own, along with the hang ups she had about relationships.

If we survived tonight, that girl and I were sitting in the pinked out room that looked like a certain panther got toey with a paint brush, and hashing it out.

Right before I fucked her to sleep, and not in the boring way.

As if the girl wasn't complicated enough without tonight's clusterfuck in the making ready to burst from the wings.

"-ing, sir?" One of the cartel heads—I couldn't recall a name on the spot—brought me out of my day dreams and left me floundering on the back deck of a multi-million dollar yacht.

"I'm sorry. Honeymoon and all. My head is still..." I shrugged and let a goofy smile slide across my face as I caught the eye of a stocky Mexican looking man and nearly fell flat on my ass.

The one ace I had up my sleeve should I need it.

Brodie Martinez.

I wondered if Archer gave Skye the same under-cover talk I got, or if Brodie was here to babysit the newb? Right now I didn't care. I was in over my head and would take all the help I could get.

"He's got his head up something, that's for sure." The stocky long term undercover Ranger with ties to cartels going back a long way elbowed my ribs and gave me a slightly leering grin. His stare hardened, daring me not to play along.

I put on the only persona I was able to come up with at short notice: the dumb ass goofball of a man with more money than sense.

As long as Skye stayed out of trouble, I'd be able to hold onto it.

"That's what new wives are for, before they become old wives," someone said to a round of jeering laughter. "Salute." The man raised his glass, clinking mine and everyone else's as they drank their varied spirits I could barely identify, being a JD and coke boy from way back.

Brodie laughed along with them, his foot hitting the back of my calf until I joined the hilarity that went on and on. Then I made the mistake even I knew not to make. I downed my cognac in one.

It took me less than a minute for the boat to sway beneath my feet, and then I couldn't feel the rest of me at all.

I woke with numb hands linked tightly behind my back. The silver bracelets bit into my skin, but the only thing I saw before me were a pair of tits I didn't recognize right in my face.

No one likes a dirty cadaver in any case. I ignored

the warning voices in my head and looked around at the roof that told me I was somewhere inside the yacht, from the sway of the boat, rather than a luxury warehouse on the dock.

At least there's still a good chance my body would be dumped in the water.

The stripper attached to the tits in my face ground away on my lap to no avail as I stared blankly up at her.

"Come on, baby. We can have fun." She cooed, sexy like. Or maybe it was supposed to be sexy, but the girl could do with a mint yesterday and every day for the rest of my life.

"Get off me," I said softly, trying to keep a rein on my politeness.

"Can't hold his liquor, eh?" One of the men from the deck called.

I shook my head and managed to slide on my stupid ass grin that was starting to hurt, doing a head-count that told me I was outnumbered five to one. Four, if I counted Brodie.

I've attended fires that smelled better than this place.

"Come on, baby." The girl rubbed her dry crotch over my equally unresponsive lap. "You can get it up."

"Afraid not. Always was a cheap drunk." I smiled at her, letting my eyes empty of emotion. Everyone else saw a stupid honeymoon lovelorn; she saw a man who pulled bodies from fires that no longer looked human and lived the last few years having nightmares about them because I wasn't about to fess up and go to counseling, just to torture myself further.

She got a glimpse of *that* man, and she moved her string bikini clad tush fast enough that I could breathe again after a few seconds and not inhale her stale-sex scent.

Marco might like another man's slops or think himself a cuck-king, but there was no chance in hell I was putting my cock in a stripper when Skye was all that consumed me since she announced me as her bodyguard for the summer.

Since the day she first flounced down on the beach beside me.

Fucking fail there.

Hell, I hoped she was alright.

I shook my head, playing it up to the crowd of drinking men, wondering what the hell Marco's game was. "Come on, guys. I already had my bachelor's party. The stripper there could shoot things out of her pussy and hit a target."

Fortunately the stripper they set on me scampered and wasn't there to claim I was talking shit out of my ass at this point.

Stay with the character. It builds doubt.

And doubt breeds, face to face.

Those were Brodie's last words to me on the brief call we had before I took off with Skye to our new beach destination. He never told me he'd be here. Though I was grateful, I wasn't really ready for more surprises.

This was meant to be a surveillance mission, after all.

"I thought we might pay a little game of truth or dare." Marco appeared through a door at the back of the room, beyond the crowd of men who parted to let him pass. "You see, I ask you a question, and you dare me not to pull the trigger for the answer."

I kept my inane smile plastered across my face. "I don't remember this game being played quite that way. But then, maybe California's a different beast." I shrugged.

Marco didn't smile back. "I think you mean Texas, Mister Ranger. Isn't that right, Skye? Isn't this the man you had to trap in order to bring him right here, to me?"

Skye slipped out from behind Marco, her face

closed, though still stunning. "That's right," she said, robotically.

Girl needs acting lessons. Or maybe it wasn't as obvious to everyone else in the room. Her false front sure as shit was to me.

"Whatcha doing, honey?" I said, mustering a little fake cheer, and letting it drop inch by inch, as though the reality was setting in. A double whammy, really, as this situation was all sorts of FUBAR. My heart wanted to pound, but too many years of fire-fighting prevented me from losing my shit just yet.

Thank Christ, as the way she looked at me then at Marco left my blood running colder than a chilled beer in winter.

"My job, dear," she said sugary sweetly, glaring at me.

CHAPTER NINE

SKYE

Lying to Hudson wasn't quite like lying to anyone else. He didn't look all butt hurt, nor did he get that fake—I only suspected it was a fake—expression that told me I wounded him somewhere deeper inside.

No, Hudson looked at me with anger underlying that stupid ass expression he plastered over his face and refused to drop.

He better not drop it. We'd both be dead if Marco had any inkling on how badly I lied to him.

And Hudson's anger would be that much easier to weather than my ex's.

Marco's arm slithered around my waist, pulling me into him like it was a place where I'd always fit.

But that wasn't quite the reality. I used to fit against him, once. I used to trust him. And becoming a Ranger when Archer knew my history was the toughest damn thing I'd ever had to do.

Then he sent us on this godforsaken mission and I knew–*I knew*– the man hated me with everything in him.

Because he just signed my death warrant sending me right back in, and probably Hudson's, too,. That was the part that hurt, the trust we built inadvertently, despite me pushing him away as much as possible.

Okay, so I did a seriously shitty job of pushing him away because being in Hudson's arms was *nice.* And no one talks about how good *nice* is until it's ripped away. All the things you don't see and appreciate when you should, and all.

Every one of my lies to him, to his face, by omission-–they all danced between us while Marco breathed down my collar like he wanted to rip of my clothes and fuck me right in front of Hudson just to prove a point.

Knowing Marco, he probably would.

I saw the moment the penny dropped for Hudson. It wasn't pretty and I swore I heard the big man's heart break from across the room, right as

Marco's hand plunged into the neckline of the dress I should never have worn and mauled my breast without permission.

"I remember buying this dress for you," he murmured into my ear, squishing my flesh like a stress toy.

I closed my eyes and pretended to be somewhere else. A beach on Tijuana, maybe. Back in bed with Hudson. On cue my nipple hardened and Marco let out a truly horrendous groan that flushed me with embarrassment and doused my arousal all over.

"Don't touch me." I jerked away from him, fixing my dress and cast my gaze anywhere except at Hudson.

I'm sorry. I should have said something.

I should have said a lot of things.

Archer gave us a hellbent, two day shunt across the country to knock out the bugs. I used my time poorly, ignoring Hudson, cradling my hurt and fear to my chest in the most unhealthy way possible.

And look where that landed us.

Not just me, but him, too.

"I'm sorry," I muttered, still daydreaming about the cottage behind the beach.

"Don't worry, sweetheart, you will be," Marco snarled, fisting my hair and wrenching me back. "Or didn't you want to give your new boyfriend the show we planned?"

I winced, breathing hard through my nose to control myself. "There is no fucking *we*, Marco, and there hasn't been for a very long time."

He growled, snatching my hand in front of his face. "My ring used to be here. *Mine*, Skye. You understand no piece of paper can take that right from me."

I glared at my ex, my mouth set in a hard line and watched the intent to murder enter Marco's eyes. This was it, then. The reason I left him before I understood how dirty the man was and not in all the right ways. Why I walked away when he was across the country, trafficking women and drugs I didn't know about at the time and requested regularly to help put to bed once I became a Ranger.

I was told I was too close to be put on the case, and his name slipped to the bottom of the pile. One man gave me the chance, knowing I didn't want to work for him, and look how well my *wish granted* moment was turning out.

Just like history repeating itself, Marco raised a hand and slashed it across my face.

The move was so familiar I didn't flinch, didn't even feel the burn as my head snapped back until my neck kinked with the sharp action. Then the pain set in, and with it came the all too once commonplace fear that froze me in place.

"Aw, crying already?" Marco mocked me as he swiped his fingers across my numb cheeks.

"Am I?" I blinked at him, not even trying to pull away. Nausea rose up my stomach, and I fought the bile back the moment it bit my tongue. That I did have control over, if nothing else. If Marco was going to kill me tonight, I didn't want to puke on his shoes and give him the satisfaction of staining my dignity along with ending my life.

"I told you, *mine,*" he gloated, lording over me.

All just the usual day for me. Three years of relative freedom disappeared with a blink, but not before Hudson turned the tables and put his life before mine.

"But she's not yours," he said, that goofy smile still curling into his voice though I wasn't looking at him. "She's mine. Ring on her hand says so."

I closed my eyes. *You stupid fucking, brave, wonderfully goofy man.* Marco would have killed him before but now he'd take Hudson's tongue, his fingers, and probably some other part of his anatomy and feed it to him before he bled out on the yacht's deck.

"A fake ring." Marco raised his chin, glaring down his nose at the man handcuffed across the room.

A tiny twitch in Hudson's shoulders drew my attention to the man who *had* been handcuffed a moment ago.

Boy's got skills.

Maybe we weren't dead yet.

CHAPTER TEN

HUDSON

I gave Skye the same dopey grin I gave Marco, like I didn't believe the situation for a minute, but this time my gaze held a message in it.

It seemed my ace in the hole turned up on time... just as planned.

Because like Skye, Archer gave me a different mission. I just hadn't realized how in depth hers was...or how personal.

Skye stalled, her breath shortening as she watched me, and swept a hand across her back and came up empty. That didn't come as a surprise; I didn't expect her to be packing in the dress she wore.

The way the asshole had his hands on her, however...that did need addressing.

The ring on her finger might be fake but the intention wasn't. She mine to love, and I'd protect her like she was, even if she decided otherwise the minute we were out of here and the man all too familiar with her sexy as fuck body. I Kept that stupid ass expression on as I loosened the handcuffs around my wrists. A pro of having a boss who was an ex-cop for many decades before he switched services. That man taught us all sorts of little tricks, and right now I was damn glad of that one.

My helping hand shifted behind Marco. Thanks to Skye's breasts suddenly pressed to his chest and the paw she allowed to grope her ass, he didn't notice the speed a big man can move at, or the gun pressed to the back of his head. Brodie nodded to me and disappeared back into the shadows. It seemed that was the man's natural habitat.

Right now, this was my rodeo. If I fucked up, he was there to clean up the mess–not save my ass.

"Let the pretty girl go, and we only have a small problem." I dangled the handcuffs in front of Marco's face.

Skye huffed a laugh. "Give me those." She jumped for them and Marco spun, his hand on her waist and his other in his pocket.

I didn't think twice. I fired.

He stood before me, a blank look on his face before his body crumpled, a hole decorating his temple.

"Born and bred in Texas," I said softly.

My gaze caught and held Skye's as someone cheered behind us. I didn't hear anything else while Brodie worked crowd control. I had no idea if I was headed for jail but the concept of not seeing Skye again hurt more than anything else.

Ignoring any threat around us, I reached for her and for once, she came to me without a fight, letting me claim her mouth in a kiss bred by pure desperation on a party night at Love Beach.

Three hours later and with a lot of repetition on our respective stories, Skye and I were back in our pink as fuck apartment at Garden House. Brodie pulled rank, which sat well with the FBI agent who also lurked on the yacht, and things moved quickly after that.

Apparently Archer had a deal with an undercover cop and slipped us into an ongoing investigation on Marco Torrino...with slightly unexpected results. No one planned for more than an arrest to take place, but Skye became the wild card Marco apparently obsessed about for years once they split. And now I was left with a shaking girl who refused to talk or do anything else than let me hold and kiss her.

Hey, it was a start. I'd take that, considering I just killed the last man she was with on any permanent basis, from what she said to the local cops But she didn't say anything else to me. At least, not yet.

Skye shifted in my arms, burrowing closer. "Winungging?" she asked into my shirt.

I'd go with it, needing the skin to skin contact, but I didn't think she'd appreciate that after the way her ex mauled at her.

"Say that again?" I asked softly, stroking her hair.

"I said," –she came up for air– "why aren't you running all the way back to Texas without me?"

I frowned, still playing with her hair. Soft curls twirled around my finger and I gave an experiment tug, drawing her closer. "Why would I run?"

"Because I'm toxic to everything I touch." She frowned back at me. "You saw me with Marco. I haven't apologized. But you saved my life and I'm..."

"In shock," I supplied, keeping my voice low and

tucking her body into mine. "Right now, all I want is my girl safe. If that means not talking, then I'll wait until you want to." *If* she wanted to talk. There was no guarantee and no way I'd push her before she was ready.

Archer gave me that tip back in his office, and it was a damn fine one.

"Why are you so *nice*," she asked desperately, reaching up to trace her fingers along my jaw.

The light caress was the sweetest thing I'd ever experienced. It didn't take long before she arched up, offering me her mouth as consolation for the words that weren't coming out. I took that second prize and ran with it.

Pink bear rug be damned, I rolled her onto her back, stretching my body along hers and kissed her until she softened beneath me. My mind was full of conflict, the need to say something–anything–about what happened on the boat killing me but the moment I opened my mouth she shut it for me.

"Not now. Not yet," she whispered. "Just... forgot. Everything."

"Not you," I whispered, cupping her jaw and sliding my tongue into her mouth.

Her legs curled around my hips, her heels urging me to rub against her, but that need from before to have skin on skin contact drew me back. I shucked my shirt onto the floor, trailing my fingers along the terry toweling robe she threw on seconds after entering the apartment, barely letting go of my hand to rip her dress off and throwing it into a corner of the room.

"I want you closer," I murmured, staring down at her.

My girl was hurting and I'd give her anything she wanted, but right now I also needed to know I wasn't pushing her past limits she'd regret in the morning.

Like fucking the man who killed her ex. Her smarmy ex, a crook, and all the things that went along with that downward spiral, but her ex all the same.

"Inside me," she begged softly. "Please, Hudson. Just...for now. I need you."

My heart ached at the pain lacing her words, and what she wasn't saying.

This thing wouldn't be permanent. I got that from the desperation in her eyes. But I wanted her so damn bad that temporary would do.

For now.

I'd work on a future version of us after I cleaned the fear and tension and pain from her face, the shadows that lingered behind her eyes.

Before she crumpled on me, I worked my fingers through the knot on her towel, pulled her robe open and dipped my head to lick her breasts. Sucked on them. Marked her in ways that wouldn't easily fade.

She let me.

There's hope.

Her finger curled through my hair, tugging my head up.

"You want me to stop, princess?" I rolled her nipple between my thumb and forefinger until she moaned, and slid lower, kissing along her stomach. "Tell me to stop, Skye." *Before I fall head over fucking heels for you.*

Too late.

I watched her face as I licked her gushing hot slit, loving the way her hips rolled up with every touch. Her head flung back, and she knotted her hands in my hair, riding my face. My cock strained in my jeans, but now had to be about calming her, not satisfying a need that was never going to pass whether she let me fuck her now or any other time.

She was my girl. My one. My California and Texan hearts slammed together in my chest as her thighs clamped around my head. She came hard on my tongue, gushing hot cream on my lips. I cleaned her slowly, letting her come down and raised my head to find her fingers out of my hair and tangled in my own.

I raised them over her head gently, catching both with one hand. Hers were so much smaller, so fragile though I knew she'd hate to hear it.

"Is this okay?" I hesitated before crossing her wrists and pressing down to hold her in place while I worked on my belt.

"It is with you." I swore her eyes glowed as she gazed up at me, her lips parted.

"Fuck," I muttered, leaning down to kiss her hard and pinned her in place. "You tell me it's too much and I'll—"

"It's not. Promise, she whispered, reaching to touch me and guide my cock between her legs.

Her heat enveloped me and my groan answered hers as I slid inside her, not stopping until I was balls deep and aching to fill her with my seed.

"Don't promise what you can't control," I said roughly, slamming my hips down again and again.

She didn't fight me once, arching up to match me. Her heels dug into my ass as I worked her over, urging me deep, harder.

Rougher.

Sweat beaded between us as I obeyed, taking us to a place where no one else existed, where nothing could hurt her. And when she screamed into my chest she took me with her, her sweet pussy milking me endlessly.

I followed willingly to the woman I fell for back in a beach in another town and chased across the country for a second chance at love on a beach.

CHAPTER ELEVEN

SKYE

I curled on Hudson's chest, listening to his heart slow its frantic pace. My thighs were sticky, and he hadn't made an effort to clean me but I got it. And...I kinda of liked the marks he left on me, something I never liked from anyone else, and certainly not–

My eyes squeezed shut as I burrowed into his chest and let out a horrifyingly weak and pitiful sound.

"It's okay. He can't hurt you anymore. Promise." Hudson's finger stroking my hair never wavered.

"I know. I just hate that he still takes up space in my head."

"Want me to remove that for you?" Before I could take another breath I was on my back, staring up into the face of the man prepared to do anything to make me happy.

Little did he seem to know that he'd already done that—removed the threat to my existence that always hung over me.

When Archer gave me my assignment, I shook my head. "No. No fucking way. Sir,' I spat placing the folder back on his desk. "I won't be involved with him again."

"But you have asked to fix the problem he presented in the past. What changed?" Archer asked, ignoring the rejected case file.

"This is putting me right in with him. Rebuilding trust like what we had was— that it was alright. This is far from okay."

Archer nodded, steeling his fingers. "You're right. It's not alright. Do you know how many women have died because of him? Indirectly, some," he ignored my gasp. "Others, because he tired of them, or they talked about his business. You thought he was bad, Skye, but the truth is he's trafficked women, drugs and ruined more lives than either of us can count on both hands. Are you prepared to let that slide?"

He held my gaze and I was the first to answer.

"No, sir. I'm not."

I kissed Hudson, snapping us both out of a place where we were lost in our heads and brought us back by complete accident. "I want a lot of things, Hudson, but I don't think I can have nice things." I offered him a sad smile. "Like you."

The best you'll get from me is a shitty partner who might fold at the worst time.

"What if I want something else?" Hudson wrapped me tight in his arms, tangling his legs around mine until I wasn't sure where he began, and I ended. "What if I think we're okay for more?"

His eyes begged me to give this a try and my traitorous heart ached to say *yes*.

"No." I shook my head. "Tonight can't happen again."

Hudson reared back, a hard look on his face. "You're right. It can't." He pushed back from me, leaving me in a pile of fake polyester bear fur, trembling a little from the force of our lovemaking.

Because Hudson didn't fuck No matter what he said, his sort of love started fun and got heavy fast. Really fast.

And I lived on a slow lane to solitude somewhere. Being caught up with him wasn't the best thing for either of us. And yet, I wanted him.

"Hudson?" I grabbed a crochet pink blanket—so,

so much pink–and wrapped it around myself. Not that it covered much, but that wasn't the point. "I'm sorry."

He laughed hollowly, raking a hand through his hair. "It should be me saying that to you." His hands trembled, his stance rigid, and I realized how much he'd hidden from me in order to take away my pain.

My heart melted a little.

Okay, a lot.

He paced the room, butt naked and incredible. The man's physique was beyond cut. He was powerful in every way, and none of the muscle was for decoration. I knew that now. Plus, the man had speed, determination, tenacity, love...what was I saying no to at this point?

His pacing grew agitated, his turns on the thick pile–yeah, pink–carpet leaving heavy indents as he stalked across the length of the room and back. It was the first time I'd seen him lose his shit, and I hated it. Wanted to fix him.

So I did the thing I thought he wanted most.

"Hudson, stop," I said quietly.

He spun on his heel, staring down at me with a hard, closed face. "You know I gave you everything. *Everything*, Skye. And my heart–fuck," he muttered rubbing his chest like he could remove the ache that tore him up from the inside.

I sympathized. Mine was the same.

"Come here," I whispered, unwrapping the blanket, and getting on my hands and knees to crawl to him. I kept it sexy, but I wanted him to see the lack of threat, what I was willing to put aside for him.

I had no idea how this would work; *if* it would work, but suddenly I saw what had been right in front of me the entire time and somehow missed it.

Missed *him*.

But he saw me when I needed him, and now I had to return that favour.

He knelt before me, hauled me up his body, frowning at me. "You shouldn't be down there."

"But it seemed like the right thing to do." I shrugged, looping my wrists behind his neck and settling over him.

Large hands caught my hips firmly and pulled me right into him, leaving no space between us. "Damn, you feel good, girl. You gonna give this thing a go? Or was that the last time I got to touch you like this?" he squeezed my ass, digging his fingers right in.

A breath whooshed from me, along with a mewl. I snapped my mouth shut and gave him a hard look. "No more freebies for you, fireboy."

"That's Ranger, princess. Just like you." He kissed me quick and drew back just as suddenly.

My heart thumped hard, and heat rose in my chest. "Do it again, but slower," I whispered. "And maybe we can find out just how long summer really lasts."

His smile turned sinful as he lifted me up and set me back down, right on top of the hard length that impaled me until I moaned his name against his mouth.

And then everything was long and slow for a damn long time.

I loved it. Him. Maybe that sort of love could cover a world of hurts, despite being so freaking scary. But with him I'd try it. Maybe for a real long time. He twirled the ring on my finger I forgot to take off, and gave me a hard squeeze.

"If I take this off now, it won't be long before it's back on," he promised darkly, before he began to move and I forgot all the arguments that could wait for the road trip back home to Texas.

Cliche? Maybe. But remember, ladies. If you've got a man who's willing to kneel for you, he thinks you're a queen.

Take that crown and be worthy of it. He'll never stop kneeling.

Thank you for reading

Thank you so much for reading!!
More than one easter egg from my Texan Devils
series floats around in Hudson and Skye's story, but
no Texas Rangers were harmed in the making of it...
at least, so far. This book runs concurrently with
RANGER'S STORM as the unit begins to undergo
a change of guard.
If you want to catch the whole series, start with
Andy and Ella's in my favorite second chance
romance of all time in RANGER'S WISH.
TEXAN DEVILS is also a crossover series with
RED HART RANCH.
Catch Archer in his own books:
SNOW ON THE RANGE (RHR book 1)

RANGER'S WRATH (TD book 5)
Mistletoe on the Range (forthcoming)

ABOUT THE AUTHOR

USA Today Bestselling author Sofia Aves writes fast-paced police romances, sizzling military units, steamy cowboys with a Montana backdrop and the occasional cheeky god. Married to a veteran, she often tackles topics of PTSD and reintegration and has a soft spot for all who work in uniform. Sofia writes kidlit for charity and has over one hundred and fifty publications across four not-so-super-secret pen names.

Sofia is a mum of three crazies in a returned veteran household and has an overly large fur baby who thinks she's a teacup puppy. After eighteen years of planning and dreaming, Sofia and her husband put the finishing touches on their very own alpaca park, Lorendel. Sofia lives near Brisbane, Australia.

www.sofiaves.com

Read Sofia's Series

Blue Blooded Brothers
 Collision
 Politics & Paperwork
Blindsided
Sentinel
Mugshots & Candy Canes
Impact
Reckoning

Red Hart Ranch
 Snow on the Range
 Siren on the Range
 Sundown on the Range
 Spirit on the Range

Ash on the Range (2025)
Mistletoe on the Range (2025)
Forgotten Mountain Man

Texan Devils

Ranger's Wish
Ranger Bedevilled
Ranger's Passion
Ranger's Fury
Ranger's Wrath
Ranger's Storm
Snapdragons & Seductions
Summer with a Ranger
Merry with a Ranger

Playing to Win

Off Boarding
Vicious Slash
Zero Pointer
Off Stage Fling

Rippton Allstars

Crushing It

Glacial Force

Rippton Creatives
Study Games
Make Me, Break Me
Twisted Obsession
Spring Break with a Mafia Prince
A Royally Fake French Menage

Jericho Chimeras
Puck Me Always
Puck My Heart
Puck me Sideways

Z Boys
King
Joker
Hearts
Ace
Mayhem & Mistletoe
Ruski

.   .   .

Fast Track to Love
>   Speed Trap

Klauss Brothers
>   Zander
>   Keegan

Gallo Empire *with Jade Marshall*
>   Splintered Vows
>   Fractured Vows
>   Fierce Vows
>   Savage Covenant

Rom Coms
>   She's A Hot Christmas Mess
>   Boats, Moats and Root Beer Floats

Writing Romantasy as
>   **SOFIA SHELLEY**
>   Dead Poets Sorority

· · ·

Writing Reverse Harem Dark Romance as
DOVE PRIEST
Recurve Ridge

Kidlit writing as
JO SEYSENER
The OCD Elf
The OCD Elf's Great Reindeer Calamity
Greg and the Egg

writing YA as
JOSS PHOENIX
Alchem Academy (2025)

Writing spicy paranormal romance as
RAVEN HUSH

Club Fray
Darkest Desires
Purge
Kidnapped By Claws
Ruin

. . .

Shadow Lords

Sinner's End

Heaven's Gate (2026)

Monster Brides

Phoenix's Eternal Flame

Kraken's Vow

Krampus' Christmas Bride

Silent Sentinels Duet

Reflections of Silence

Echoes in the Void

Monsters In New York

Feral Moon Rising (2025)